Colette Stone and Elizabeth Stone

Illustrator
Andhika Abhiramadhan

Editor
John Hansen

This book belongs to

....

....

I see someone else staring back at me.

When I smile at them, they smile at me too. When I reach out to touch them, they reach out too.

Who is this person, is it me? Is it you? Where have they come from, what do they do?

I want to know more, so I look behind.
I cannot see them.
They are nowhere in sight.

I look in mirror and again,
they are there, looking at me,
with the same messy hair.

That are just the same colour brown as mine.

They are even wearing the same shirt and pants.
And they even do the same silly dance.

Does the child have a sweet smile and laugh?
Yes! Just like me.

Does the child in the mirror jump and dance? Yes! Just like me.

Nobody else, nobody but me.
I love who I am and who I am going to be.